WHAT DOES IT DO?
BULLDOZER

BY GAETANO CAPICI

CHERRY LAKE
Publishing

Published in the United States of America by Cherry Lake Publishing
Ann Arbor, Michigan
www.cherrylakepublishing.com

Content Adviser: Louis Teel, Professor of Heavy Equipment, Central Arizona College
Reading Adviser: Cecilia Minden-Cupp, PhD, Literacy Consultant

Photo Credits: Cover and page 1, ©Artem Rudik/Shutterstock, Inc.; page 5, ©Stanislav Komogorov/Shutterstock, Inc.; page 7, ©ownway/Shutterstock, Inc.; page 9, ©Jose Gil/Shutterstock, Inc.; page 11, ©Darryl Brooks/Shutterstock, Inc.; page 13, ©VR Photos/Shutterstock, Inc.; page 15, ©M. A. Battilana/Alamy; page 17, ©Bonita R. Cheshier/Shutterstock, Inc.; page 19, ©Jim Zuckerman/Alamy; page 21, ©Sergey Kozoderov/Shutterstock, Inc.

LIBRARY OF CONGRESS CATALOGING-IN-PUBLICATION DATA
Capici, Gaetano, 1985–
What does it do? Bulldozer/by Gaetano Capici.
p. cm.—(Community connections)
Includes bibliographical references and index.
ISBN-13: 978-1-60279-972-1 (lib. bdg.)
ISBN-10: 1-60279-972-5 (lib. bdg.)
1. Bulldozers—Juvenile literature. I. Title. II. Title: Bulldozer. III. Series.
TA725.C35 2011
624.1'52—dc22 2010023580

Cherry Lake Publishing would like to acknowledge the work of The Partnership for 21st Century Skills. Please visit *www.21stcenturyskills.org* for more information.

Printed in the United States of America
Corporate Graphics Inc.
January 2011
CLSP08

BULLDOZER

CONTENTS

4 Powerful Pushers

10 Moving Around

14 Many Jobs

18 Special Machines

22 Glossary

23 Find Out More

24 Index

24 About the Author

WHAT DOES IT DO?

POWERFUL PUSHERS

Buzz! Clank! A roaring bulldozer is hard at work. Have you ever seen a bulldozer?

A bulldozer has a special type of blade. It hooks onto a tractor. The whole machine is called a bulldozer. Bulldozers do many jobs. They are used in many building **projects**.

Bulldozers are used for many kinds of jobs.

Bulldozers are **earthmovers**. They are used to push many things. Different blades do different jobs. Some blades make the ground **level**. Other blades move rocks and dirt.

A bulldozer may also have a tool called a **ripper**. It is at the back of the machine. A ripper's strong metal claws break up hard ground.

Bulldozers can clear the way for builders to start working.

The ripper is lowered toward the ground. A driver inside the bulldozer then drives forward. The ripper tears into the ground, breaking it up. The ripper is raised.

Now the blade can get back to work. It pushes the rocks and dirt.

Can you see the ripper that is used to break up the soil?

MAKE A GUESS!

Some bulldozers are very large. How heavy are the biggest bulldozers? Guess how much they weigh. You may find the answer in library books. You can look online, too. Was your guess correct?

MOVING AROUND

Some bulldozers have special tires. Most move on **crawler tracks**. The tracks are like large belts. The belts turn around special frames. As they turn, the machine moves.

Bulldozers might be needed in sandy or muddy spots. Bulldozers with normal tires might get stuck.

Bumps in the crawler tracks help keep the bulldozer from sliding or getting stuck.

Tracks help the bulldozer move over many types of ground. They also help it climb bumpy hills.

The tracks are wide. They help spread the weight of the bulldozer. This is important. No one wants the bulldozer to sink in muddy ground!

Crawler tracks help bulldozers go wherever they are needed.

LOOK!

Take a good look at a bulldozer's crawler tracks. They are good at **gripping** the ground. What do you think the tracks are made of? If you said metal, you are right! What other big machines have tracks like these?

MANY JOBS

Does the job call for dumping or pushing a **load**? A bulldozer can do the job! Bulldozers clear space for roads and homes.

Bulldozers also help workers build **structures** such as dams. Sometimes, bulldozers knock down walls or buildings. They may also remove trees.

Bulldozers can help workers knock down buildings.

CAT

You might find bulldozers at trash dumps. They help push and bury trash. Bulldozers can also level out the sand on beaches. Others save the day after bad snowstorms. They clear away snow. Bulldozers may also do some digging jobs.

Trucks carry bulldozers from one job site to another.

THINK!

Large trucks bring bulldozers from one **construction site** to the next. Some bulldozers are taken apart first. The parts are carried on more than one truck. Why do you think that is? Think about bulldozers. Are they heavy? Do they move fast?

SPECIAL MACHINES

Running a bulldozer is harder than driving a car. A bulldozer driver sits in a cab. She uses special controls to move the parts. She knows how to turn the tractor in different directions.

Bulldozer drivers are trained to safely operate these big machines.

Picture a construction site for a new road. A bulldozer is pushing earth into big piles. It is clearing space.

Soon, different machines will be able to do their jobs at the site. They all do their part to finish the project. Bulldozers are important tools for a building team!

Bulldozers help build the roads and buildings we use every day!

GLOSSARY

construction site (kuhn-STRUHK-shuhn SITE) an area where something is being built

crawler tracks (KRAW-lur TRAKSS) special bands or belts used to move some machines

earthmovers (URTH-moo-vurz) machines used to move or dig into large amounts of soil and rock

gripping (GRIP-ing) keeping a strong hold on something without slipping

level (LEV-uhl) flat and even

load (LOHD) something heavy that is carried or pushed

projects (PROJ-ektss) tasks that require a lot of work and planning

ripper (RIP-ur) a tool used to break up dirt in hard ground

structures (STRUHK-churz) things that have been built

FIND OUT MORE

BOOKS

Alinas, Marv. *Bulldozers*. Mankato, MN: Child's World, 2008.

Tourville, Amanda Doering. *Bulldozers*. Edina, MN: Magic Wagon, 2009.

WEB SITES

Activity TV—Crafts: Bulldozer
www.activitytv.com/683-bulldozer
Discover how to make a toy bulldozer out of household items.

Kikki's Workshop—Bulldozer
www.kenkenkikki.jp/zukan/e_bull_h00.html
Find helpful facts and photos of bulldozers at this site.

INDEX

blades, 4, 6, 8

cabs, 18
claws, 6
controls, 18
crawler tracks, 10, 12, 13

dirt, 6, 8
drivers, 8, 18

earthmovers, 6

hills, 12

leveling, 6, 16

moving, 10, 12, 17, 18
mud, 10, 12

projects, 4, 20

rippers, 6, 8
rocks, 6, 8

sand, 10, 16

tires, 10
tractors, 4, 18
trucks, 17

weight, 9, 12

ABOUT THE AUTHOR

Gaetano Capici graduated from DePaul University with bachelor's degrees in English and Spanish. He lives near Chicago, Illinois.